Veterans Day, on November 11, honors all U.S. military veterans. It began as Armistice Day in 1919 to mark the end of World War I and was renamed in 1954 to recognize veterans from all wars. The day celebrates veterans with ceremonies and parades.

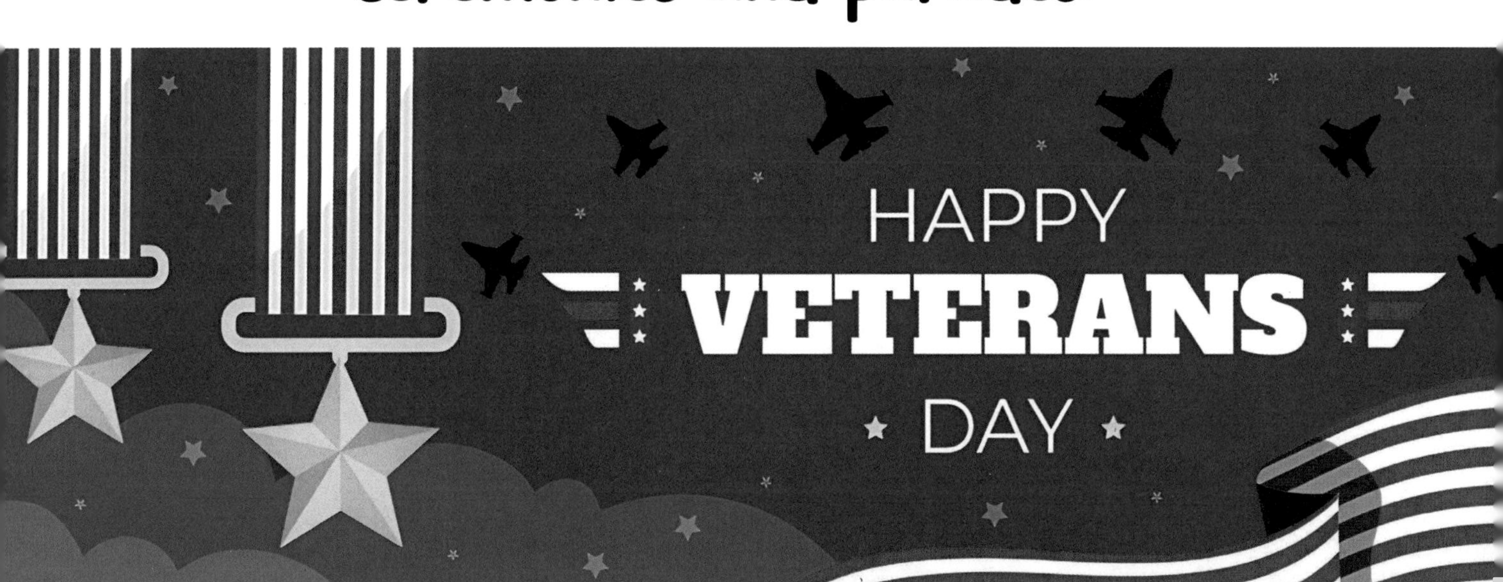

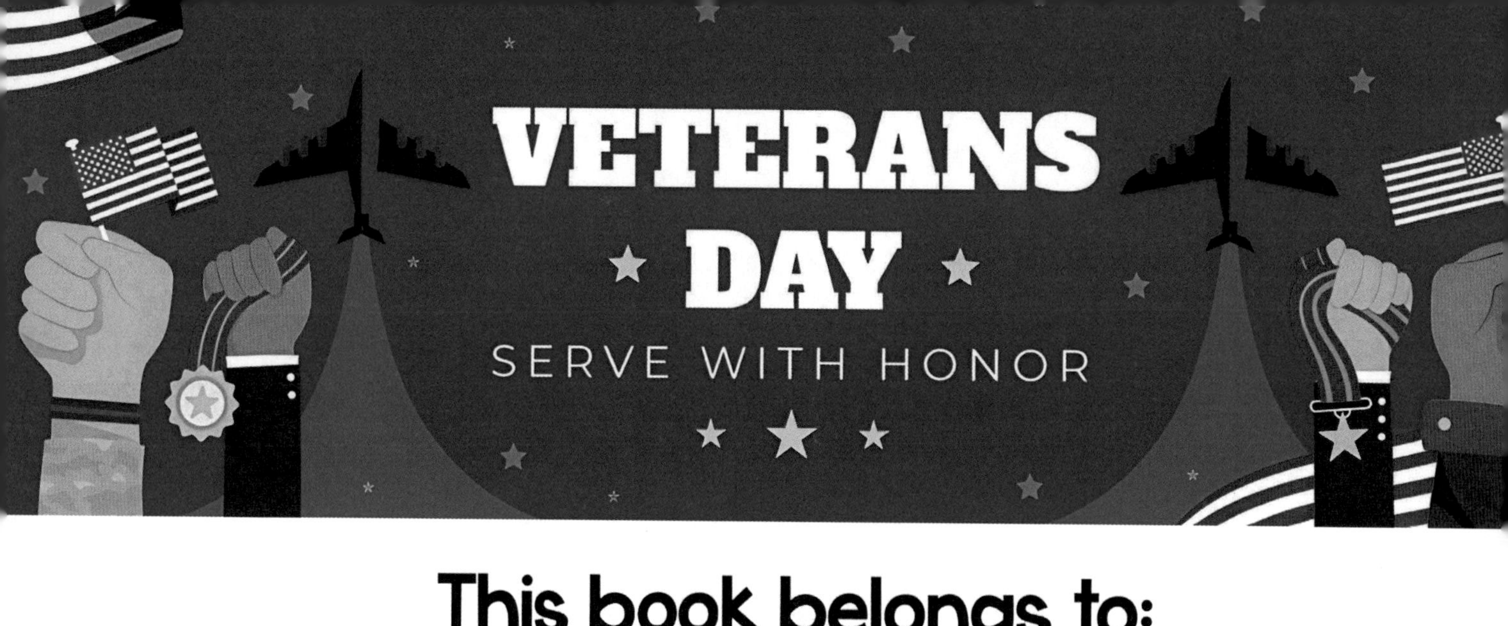


This book belongs to:

Emma and Jack join Grandpa Joe on Veterans Day to learn about his military past, the meaning of heroism, and his exciting adventures.

Emma and her brother Jack received a letter in their mailbox, covered in red, white, and blue stars. It was from their Grandpa Joe, inviting them on a special adventure to celebrate Veterans Day. Grandpa Joe was a retired soldier, and he loved sharing stories about his time serving the country. The kids were excited but curious—what did Grandpa have planned?

The kids packed their backpacks, bringing their notebooks and pencils to write down anything interesting Grandpa might tell them. Their mom dropped them off at Grandpa's house a small home filled with medals, photographs, and American flags. Grandpa greeted them with a big hug and a sparkle in his eye. "Ready for an adventure, troops?"
he asked with a grin.

Grandpa Joe led Emma and Jack to the backyard, where he had set up a small tent and placed a map on a wooden table. "Today," he said, pointing at the map, "we're going to learn all about what it means to be a hero, and you two are my explorers! " Emma and Jack beamed with excitement as Grandpa showed them the first spot they would visit.

They arrived at the first spot Grandpa had planned, an old oak tree with medals hanging from its branches. Grandpa Joe carefully took one down and showed it to the kids. "This is the Purple Heart," he explained. "It's given to soldiers who were hurt while trying to help others." Emma and Jack listened carefully, awed by the shiny medal in his hand.

Grandpa shared stories of his friends who had received this medal. He told them about brave soldiers who had helped each other during tough times. "They were all heroes," he said, his voice full of pride. The kids looked up at Grandpa, imagining all the brave people he had known and the sacrifices they'd made.

As they moved to another part of the backyard, Grandpa Joe showed them the Medal of Honor. "This is given to people who do something incredibly brave," he explained, holding it out. Emma and Jack were amazed. "Wow, Grandpa, you really knew so many heroes!" Emma exclaimed, feeling inspired.

The next stop on Grandpa's adventure was a small memorial he'd set up with photos of his friends from his time in the military. "These are my buddies," he said, pointing to each picture with a fond smile. "They might be gone, but they'll always be remembered." Emma and Jack were quiet, feeling the importance of this moment.

Grandpa told them stories about each friend, from funny moments to acts of bravery that saved lives. Emma and Jack were amazed at how each person had their own special story. Grandpa's friends had come from different places, but they were all like family to him. "We called each other 'brothers,'" he explained.

Before they left, Grandpa asked them to stand quietly and think about the bravery of all soldiers. Emma and Jack closed their eyes, imagining the courage of Grandpa's friends. Grandpa placed his hand on their shoulders. "You see, being a hero isn't just about bravery—it's about friendship, too."

At the end of the day, Grandpa led them back to the backyard where he had a surprise waiting. A little red, white, and blue cake was sitting on a picnic table with the words, "Thank you, heroes!" written in icing. Grandpa handed them each a small flag. "This is to remember today and all the brave people we talked about."

Thank you,
heroes!

As they enjoyed the cake, Grandpa said, "I want you both to remember that you don't have to be a soldier to be a hero. Helping others and being kind are the most important things." Emma and Jack looked at Grandpa with new respect, understanding that heroes come in many forms.

When it was time to go, Grandpa hugged them tight. "I'm proud of you both," he said. As they waved goodbye, Emma and Jack left with full hearts, knowing this was a Veterans Day they'd never forget. Grandpa's stories had left a lasting mark on them, showing them what true heroism means.

# QUIZ

# *Circle The Correct aswer*

What did Emma and Jack find in their mailbox that started their adventure?

A) A medal from Grandpa

B) A letter

C) A small flag

What special item did Grandpa Joe show Emma and Jack that represented bravery in the military?

A) A compass

B) A Medal of Honor

C) A flag

Why did Grandpa Joe set up a memorial with photos of his friends?

A) To remember and honor his friends who served

B) To show Emma and Jack how medals are awarded

C) To teach them about collecting

What did Grandpa Joe and the kids do at the end of the day to celebrate?

A) Ate a cake with "Thank you, heroes!" on it

B) Took a trip to a museum

C) Made a new flag for the yard